Miss Mary's Christmas Mittens

Trinka Hakes Noble

ILLUSTRATED BY Renée Andriani

PUBLISHED by SLEEPING BEAR PRESS™

Miss Mary was everyone's favorite teacher.

She loved to knit, and her brightly colored outfits always made her students smile. Her lessons were fun and made learning easy.

School was a happy place with Miss Mary.

Just before Christmas vacation, the first snow fell.

On her way to school, Miss Mary tested the snow for good packing. She designed amazing snowmen and snow angels in her head.

We'll have an extra-long recess today since it's our last day before Christmas break, she thought. It will be so much fun!

Soon lessons were done.

"It's recess time!" announced Miss Mary excitedly.

"Now bundle up, everyone!"

Miss Mary wrapped herself up in her coat, scarf, hat,
and gloves while her class quickly lined up at the door.

But recess was *not* fun.

The snow angels didn't have wings.

The snowmen were lopsided or missing their heads.

And the playground hockey game didn't last long.

Why?

Everyone's cold hands were tucked in their coat pockets.

Oh my, thought Miss Mary, *they don't have any mittens.*
Well, I'll knit them warm mittens.
I can give them as Christmas presents!

After school, Miss Mary rushed to the store to buy yarn.
But the shelves were empty.

"Christmas is just days away and I need to knit mittens for gifts!
Why don't you have any yarn?" Miss Mary asked the store owner.

"I'm sorry, Miss Mary. I'm afraid we've run out and
we won't have any more deliveries before Christmas."

As Miss Mary sadly walked home, something tickled her nose.

"What's this?" She gave it a tug. "Aha!" She laughed.

Miss Mary ran home and unraveled her hat, scarf, and gloves.

"But that's not enough for twenty pairs of mittens," she said.

Soon her sweater and socks became a heap of yarn.

"But I need more!" she cried, and began
pulling clothes from her closet to unravel.

"STILL NOT ENOUGH!" she shouted.

There went her slippers, pot holders, and afghan.
More and more and more, until the piles of yarn
seemed almost as high as snowdrifts.

Then Miss Mary wound balls of yarn late into the night.

The next morning, Miss Mary sat by her warm fire and began to knit.

"Only two days before Christmas! I must hurry!"

CLICKETY-CLACK went her needles. Knit one, purl two,
there's a cuff, now a thumb. Soon the first little pair was finished.

On her knitting needles flew! Now a second pair was done.
Just eighteen more to go.

CLICKETY-CLACK, CLACKITY-CLICK,
CLICKETY-CLACK-CLACK-CLACK!

Miss Mary knitted faster and faster all that day and the next.

On Christmas Eve, twenty little pairs of mittens hung in a row.
Then, with the leftover yarn, she knitted some scarves and hats, too.

Outside, silver stars sparkled over the snow as Miss Mary lovingly wrapped each gift in tissue paper and tied it with a bow.

At dawn on Christmas morning, Miss Mary tiptoed around town, leaving each student their gift.

On Christmas Day, the happy sounds of children playing outdoors could be heard all over town, and soon . . .

little helpers swept porches and
shoveled sidewalks.

Skaters and hockey players went round
and round on frozen ponds.

And beautiful snow angels were seen everywhere.

But the best thing of all appeared in Miss Mary's front yard.

"Come look,
Miss Mary!"

Miss Mary felt as warm inside as a **Christmas mitten.**

A Special Mitten Ornament for You to Knit!

Miss Mary showed her students how much she cared for them by knitting them mittens. Here is a mitten ornament you can knit for someone special in your life.

KNITTING PATTERN COURTESY of RED HEART & YARNSPIRATIONS.COM

THINGS YOU'LL NEED TO KNOW BEFORE YOU BEGIN:

Measurement: Approx 2½" [6 cm] wide, excluding thumb x 4" [10 cm] long.

Gauge: 17 sts and 23 rows = 4" [10 cm] in stocking st.

Materials You Will Need:
- Yarn: 1 skein of desired color (7 oz/198 g; 364 yds/333 m)
- Size U.S. 8 (5 mm) knitting needles
- Size U.S. D/3 (3.25 mm) crochet hook or size needed to obtain gauge
- Yarn needle
- Stitch holder

Abbreviations

Alt = Alternate(ing) | **Approx** = Approximately | **Beg** = Beginning | **Ch** = Chain(s) | **K** = Knit | **K2tog** = Knit next 2 stitches together | **Kfb** = Increase 1 stitch by knitting into front and back of next stitch | **P** = Purl | **P2tog** = Purl next 2 stitches together | **Rem** = Remaining | **Rep** = Repeat | **RS** = Right side | **Sl st** = Slip stitch | **St(s)** = Stitch(es) | **WS** = Wrong side

Mitten Knitting Instructions (Make 2)

Cuff Ribbing
Cast on 22 sts.
1st row: (RS). *K1. P1. Rep from * to end of row.
Rep this row of (K1. P1) ribbing 5 times more.

Work 2 rows stocking st (Knit on RS rows. Purl on WS rows).

Shape Thumb: 1st row: (RS). K10. (Kfb) twice. K10. 24 sts.
2nd and alt rows: Purl.
3rd row: K10. Kfb. K2. Kfb. K10. 26 sts.
5th row: K10. Kfb. K4. Kfb. K10. 28 sts.
6th row: Purl.

Divide for Thumb: 1st row: (RS). K10. Cast on 2 sts. Place next 8 sts on a st holder.
K10. 22 sts. Work 9 rows stocking st.

Shape Top: 1st row: (RS). (K2tog) 11 times. 11 sts.
2nd row: (P2tog) 5 times. P1. Cut yarn, leaving a long end. Weave through rem 6 sts.
Pull tightly to secure.

Thumb
Slip 8 sts from st holder onto needle.
1st row: (RS). Kfb. K6. Kfb. 10 sts.
Work even for 3 rows stocking st.

Next row: (K2tog) 5 times. Cut yarn leaving a long end. Weave through rem 5 sts.
Pull tightly and fasten.

FINISHING
Sew top and thumb seams. Sew thumb base to hand. With crochet hook, join yarn with
sl st at thumb side of mitten at cast on edge. Ch 50. Join with sl st to other mitten at
corresponding thumb edge. Fasten off. Weave in all ends.

FOR ANOTHER HOLIDAY CRAFT IDEA FOR THE LITTLEST READERS,
Visit www.trinkahakesnoble.com/books/miss-marys-christmas-mittens/ornament/

For Ruby and Ivy,
who love snow
With love,
T.H.N.

For Judy Sue and April,
and teachers everywhere who give of themselves
—Renée

SLEEPING BEAR PRESS™

Text Copyright © 2022 Trinka Hakes Noble
Illustration Copyright © 2022 Renée Andriani
Design Copyright © 2022 Sleeping Bear Press
All rights reserved. No part of this book may be reproduced in any
manner without the express written consent of the publisher,
except in the case of brief excerpts in critical reviews and articles.
All inquiries should be addressed to:
2395 South Huron Parkway, Suite 200, Ann Arbor, MI 48104
www.sleepingbearpress.com © Sleeping Bear Press
Printed and bound in the United States
10 9 8 7 6 5 4 3 2 1
Library of Congress Cataloging-in-Publication Data
Names: Noble, Trinka Hakes, author. | Andriani, Renée, illustrator.
Title: Miss Mary's Christmas mittens / Trinka Hakes Noble ; illustrated by Renée Andriani.
Description: Ann Arbor, MI : Sleeping Bear Press, [2022] |
Audience: Ages 4-8. | Audience: Grades 2-3. | Summary: A teacher who
wants to knit mittens as Christmas gifts for her students finds a
creative solution when she runs into a yarn shortage.
Identifiers: LCCN 2022003615 | ISBN 9781534111677 (hardcover)
Subjects: CYAC: Teachers—Fiction. | Mittens—Fiction. | Knitting—Fiction.
| Kindness—Fiction. | Christmas—Fiction. | LCGFT: Picture books.
Classification: LCC PZ7.N6715 Mi 2022 | DDC [E]—dc23
LC record available at https://lccn.loc.gov/2022003615